D1265734

WONDER BOOKS®

Forests

A Level Two Reader

By Cynthia Klingel and Robert B. Noyed

The
Child's World®

Plants and animals live in many different places. One of these places is the forest.

The forest has many trees.
Trees can be very tall. Many
trees have leaves.

Other trees have green needles instead of leaves. Some trees with needles are called pine trees.

The ground in the forest is covered with plants. Many of these plants are green. Some of them have flowers or berries.

Many birds live in the trees of the forest. Owls are birds that live in some forests. Songbirds, eagles, and hawks live in forests, too.

Many other animals live in the forest. Deer eat the forest plants.

Bears live in some forests. Black bears eat plants and fruits. They also climb trees.

Some forest animals live in the trees. Squirrels climb the trees. They jump from branch to branch.

There are also many bugs and insects in the forest. Some insects climb on the trees. Others climb on the smaller plants.

The forest is beautiful and interesting. It is filled with animals and plants. The forest is a special place.

Index

To Find Out More

Books

George, Lindsay Barrett. *In the Woods: Who's Been Here?* New York: William Morrow, 1998.

Godwin, Laura. *Forest.* New York: HarperCollins Children's Books, 1999.

Rutten, Joshua. *Forests.* Chanhassen, Minn.: The Child's World, 1999.

Web Sites

Explore the Fantastic Forest
http://www.nationalgeographic.com/features/96/forest.html/forest.html
To take a virtual nature walk.

The Secret Forest
http://www.afseeee.org/sf/home.html
To learn about the mysteries of forest life.

Note to Parents and Educators

Welcome to The Wonders of Reading™! These books provide text at three different levels for beginning readers to practice and strengthen their reading skills. In addition, the use of nonfiction text gives readers the valuable opportunity to *read to learn*, not just to learn to read.

These leveled readers allow children to choose books at their level of reading confidence and performance. Level One books offer beginning readers simple language, word choice, and sentence structure as well as a word list. Level Two books feature slightly more difficult vocabulary, longer sentences, and longer total text. In the back of each Level Two book are an index and a list of books and Web sites for finding out more information. Level Three books continue to extend word choice and length of text. In the back of each Level Three book are a glossary, an index, and a list of books and Web sites for further research.

State and national standards in reading and language arts emphasize using nonfiction at all levels of reading development. The Wonders of Reading™ books fill the historical void in nonfiction for primary grade readers with the additional benefit of a leveled text.

About the Authors

Cynthia Klingel has worked as a high school English teacher and an elementary teacher. She is currently the curriculum director for a Minnesota school district. Writing children's books is another way for her to continue her passion for sharing the written word with children. Cynthia is a frequent visitor to the children's section of bookstores and enjoys spending time with her many friends, family, and two daughters.

Robert Noyed started his career as a newspaper reporter. Since then, he has worked in communications and public relations for more than fourteen years for a Minnesota school district. He enjoys writing books for children and finds that it brings a different feeling of challenge and accomplishment from other writing projects. He is an avid reader who also enjoys music, theater, traveling, and spending time with his wife, son, and daughter.

Published by The Child's World®, Inc.

PO Box 326
Chanhassen, MN 55317-0326
800-599-READ
www.childsworld.com

Project Coordination: Editorial Directions, Inc.
Photo Research: Alice K. Flanagan

Library of Congress Cataloging-in-Publication Data
Klingel, Cynthia Fitterer.
Forests / by Cynthia Klingel and Robert B. Noyed.
    p. cm.
ISBN 1-56766-973-5 (lib. bdg.)
1. Forest animals—Juvenile literature. 2. Forest plants—Juvenile literature.
[1. Forests.]   I. Noyed, Robert B. II. Title.
QH86 .K55 2001
578.73—dc21
                                00-013179